Hello, Pepi Nana!

By Andrew Davenport

Copyright © 2019 Moon and Me

Scholastic Children's Books,
Euston House, 24 Eversholt Street,
London NW1 1DB, UK

A division of Scholastic Ltd
London ~ New York ~ Toronto ~ Sydney ~ Auckland
Mexico City ~ New Delhi ~ Hong Kong

Published in the UK by Scholastic Ltd, 2019

ISBN 978 1407 19813 2

Printed and bound in China

2 4 6 8 10 9 7 5 3 1

The right of Andrew Davenport to be identified as the author of this work respectively has been asserted
by him in accordance with the Copyright, Designs and Patents Act, 1988.

Pepi Nana is a magical toy.
She lives in a Toy House.

"Tiddle toddle!"

Hello, Pepi Nana!

When the moon shines,
Pepi Nana wakes up.

She writes a letter and
sends it to the moon.

Who will read
Pepi Nana's letter?

Moon Baby!
Pepi Nana and Moon Baby
are best friends.

Pepi Nana loves books.
"Tiddle toddle!"

Pepi Nana shares her stories with all her friends.

Moon Baby plays his magical kalimba.

Time to go to Storyland!

Pepi Nana loves to hide
in the great big tub.

Rub-a-dub-dub,
Pepi Nana in a tub!

"Tiddle toddle!"
says Pepi Nana.
"It's raining!"

Luckily, everybody
can fit under
Pepi Nana's
umbrella.

Pepi Nana rides on the
Tricycle-made-for-two
with her best friend
Moon Baby.

Pepi Nana loves to play
music with her friends.
What a very special guitar!

"Tiddle toddle!"

Time for tea, together.

Pepi Nana loves her friends.

Bye-bye, Moon Baby.
Until next time.

Hush, hush, it's time
to go to sleep.

Goodnight, Pepi Nana.